To Pierce and Perri – Wendy
To Mom and Dad – Matt

Copyright © 2015 by Wendy Hundere Parnell and Matt Hall

Summary: Johnny 99 has been caught racing in the street—again. Now he's in trouble with his dad—again. Wanting to assert his independence and in hopes of finding adventure, Johnny 99 leaves his hometown to travel across the country. He returns home a changed car.

Printed in the U.S.A.

Library of Congress Cataloging-In-Publication Data is available.

ISBN: 978-0-9845843-2-1

Born to Run
The Story of Johnny 99

written by **Wendy Parnell** illustrated by **Matt Hall**
inspired by the music of **Bruce Springsteen**

It was a quiet night in Lucky Town.

From the factory on E Street to the mansion on the hill,
everyone was asleep, and the town stood still.
From Thunder Road that runs the length of the town
to 57th and Tenth Avenue, there was no one around.

At home on Flamingo Lane, two cars slept without a care—
Rosalita, a pink Cadillac, and Frankie, a '57 Chevy Bel Air.

Each car happily slumbered, each working on a dream.
It was another peaceful night, or so it did seem.

Frankie and Rosalita awoke to a loud sound, a rumbling beat.
They knew in an instant it was their son, racing in the street.
Though he had been told not to more than once before,
they recognized his engine and its familiar roar.

Johnny 99 slammed on his brakes when he saw his dad.
He knew he had done wrong and that his dad would be mad.

"Let me tell you again point blank," Frankie said to his son.
"Your days of racing in the street are finished and done!"

"Awww, Dad," Johnny complained, "but I was born to run.
Can't a car like me have a little fun?
Besides, what about you, Dad? You used to race.
I've seen all the trophies you won for first place."

"Son, I do remember my glory days and how it felt to go fast.
But I didn't always win; sometimes I even came in last."

Father and son were silent a moment, both looking at the stars.
Then Frankie said to Johnny, "Is it better to go fast or to go far?
Johnny, life is not a race to be won. Remember this, please.
You want to take time to stop and smell the engine grease.
Besides, out in the street is not where you should race.
If you want to speed, you know a racetrack is the place."

"Speaking of a different place," Johnny said in reply,
"Well, Dad...." He hesitated and looked up at the sky.

"I've been thinking. Maybe it's time I left my hometown.
You know, see new things and see what else is around.
After all, I was born in the U.S.A. and so, to me, it seems
it's time I explore this so-called Land of Hope and Dreams.
I know that past the darkness on the edge of town
are roads and backstreets just waiting to be found."

Frankie sighed. "Johnny, you've got it. You can go.
But there are some things that are important for you to know.
There will be challenges," Frankie explained to his son.
"This hard land has some rough roads, and it won't all be fun.
Our big and beautiful world wears a brilliant disguise.
To be true to yourself and keep a fire within, you would be wise.
If you find yourself lost or at loose ends, stay calm;
there will always be someone who can help you along.
Oh, and one last suggestion I have for your trip:
try to leave each place better than you found it."

Hiding his sad eyes, Frankie said, "That's all, I guess.
Your mom and I will miss you and wish you the best.
Just make us the promise you will stay in touch along the way.
Let us know you're all right and that everything's OK."

So Frankie and Rosalita told Johnny bye-bye
and wished him the best on his cross-country drive.
Turning on Highway 29, Johnny disappeared from view
as adventures awaited him, both bold and new.

Johnny 99 sent postcards and letters most every day,
telling his parents what was happening as he made his way.

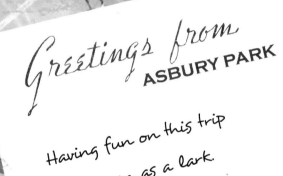

FREEHOLD
MAR 16
1 PM
1975
N.J.

Greetings from **ASBURY PARK**

Having fun on this trip
that began as a lark.
I saw the ocean,
put my tires in the sand,
went down to the pier,
even heard a great band.

Love,
Johnny

Rosa
194
Lu

PALA
FUNHOUSE
TUNNEL·OF·LOVE
MERRY-GO
TWISTE

GREETINGS
FROM

AMARILLO
POST CARD

Frankie

go Lane

USA

Dear Mom and Dad,

It's like magic here in Texas.

Cadillac Ranch is quite a sight.

You wouldn't believe all the cars

half-buried and upright!

L~

Rosalita and Frankie

1949 Flamina~

Luck~

POST CARD

R

In the small town of Marfa,

I saw some mysterious lights.

They were dancing in the dark

like spirits in the night!

Love,
Johnny

Dear Mom and Dad,

My hungry heart led me to roam
and now I'm a thousand miles
from home.

Today I saw the rising of the sun
over Galveston Bay,
blinded by the light of its
glorious rays!

Love,
Johnny

Greetings Fr

PAR

SANTA ANA, CA
JUN 20
1975

Dear Mom and Dad,

Enjoying salt air and an ocean view today,

in Southern California, down San Diego way.

As the light of day begins to fade away,

I have high hopes of visiting again some day.

Love,
Johnny

DISE

ter days
e for you!

99

/975

Dear Mom and Dad,

I got trapped in the badlands of
Nebraska in a stroke of bad luck,
when I missed my turn and got
unbelievably stuck!
The rocky ground was nearly a
wrecking ball to my offroad plans,
'til I was rescued by a state trooper
and a highway patrolman.

I love you!
Johnny

Rosalita and Frankie
1949 Flamingo Lane
Lucky Town USA

RECEIVED

PARK IN NEBRASKA

Dear Mom and Dad,

My turn to repay the kindness I had just received soon came.
The big payback occurred further on up the road in heavy rain.
Because the night was so dark with the rain pouring down,
I was unsure where I was, or what was around.

So I pulled over to wait under a sign that read "Abram's Bridge."

There was a loud thundercrack and lightning from just over the ridge.

Then without warning came the rising of the river,

so sudden it made my nuts and bolts quiver.

Lost in the flood, the bridge swallowed up, no longer there,

an empty sky in its place and the road now to nowhere!

Looking in my rearview mirror, I saw a line of cars headed my way,
cars that didn't know about the bridge and its sudden breakaway.
Turning around and facing the oncoming cars,
and countin' on a miracle and my lucky stars,
I frantically flashed my lights and honked a warning sign.
The cars all saw me and braked...

                                            ...just in the nick of time!

Johnny's parents read the last postcard with a happy sigh.

POST CARD

CORRESPONDENCE HERE

NA

R

Dear Mom and Dad,
Coming home! Can't wait!
See you on the 4th of July!

Love, your son,
Johnny

15 cents

TED!
eralded

Witnesses to that night say Johnny 99 acted swiftly and with self-less regard for his own safe-ty and that it was his courage and quick thinking that saved other cars from certain peril. Numerous reports from those were there tell of how tions kept oth-the river.

Independence Day and the whole town was there
to welcome Johnny 99 home and show him they cared.
But something seemed different about Johnny when he came into view,
as he didn't speed or rev his engine, which was unlike him and new.

"Speech! Speech!" everyone chanted to the prodigal son.
"Tell us! How was your trip? What'd you learn? Was it fun?"
Johnny took center stage as a hometown star
and gave reason to believe he was now a changed car.

Johnny hadn't prepared a speech to be read.
"So I'll just speak from my heart," Johnny slowly said.
"Youngstown, Reno, streets of Philadelphia, Atlantic City...
every place unique, interesting, and most of them pretty.
Though it was a great trip across the U.S. of A.,
I feel lucky and happy to be here today.
And while I enjoyed traveling to so many new places,
I was missing seeing all of your familiar faces.
Sherry, Billy, Mary, Sandy, Wendy, Terry—you're all here,
and of course my parents, whom I hold so dear."

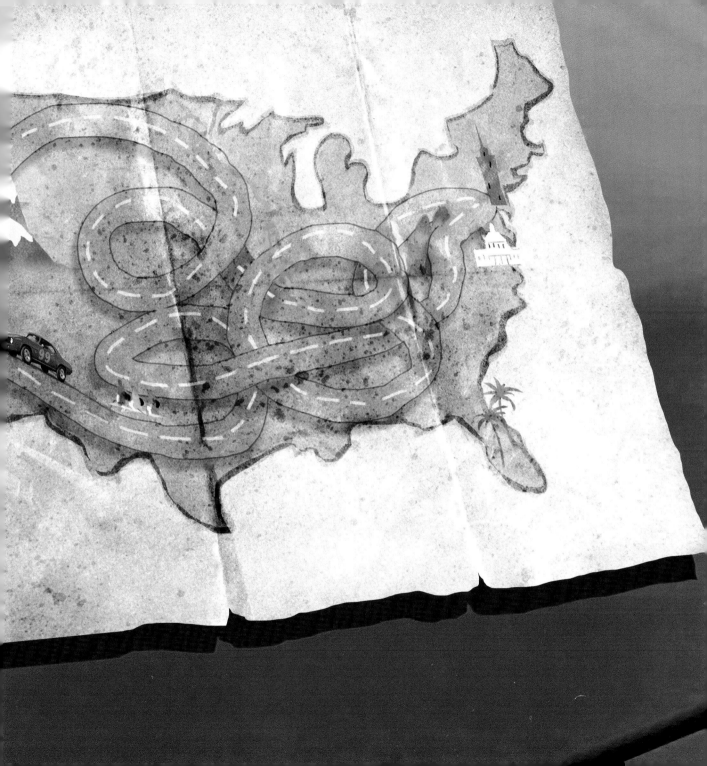

"Mom, Dad...I did a lot of growin' up on this trip, and I now realize you were right. There's something better than racing and winning first prize." Johnny excitedly shared with everyone what he now understood: "What matters most is not the trophies but what's under the hood.

"I know now it's not about being the fastest 'round the track,
that this life is less about taking and more about giving back.
The roads we share are just some of the ties that bind;
it's also the help we give without expecting in kind.
And while going fast can be fun and has its place,
I now think slowing down to enjoy the journey is the better pace.
I learned that when you love someone, you're never alone...

...and the best part about leaving is coming home."